Nouns and Have a Verbs Field Day

by **Robin Pulver**

illustrated by **Lynn Rowe Reed**

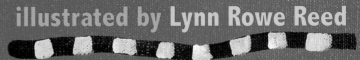

Holiday House / New York

Text copyright © 2006 by Robin Pulver
Illustrations copyright © 2006 by Lynn Rowe Reed
All Rights Reserved.
Printed and bound in 11/09 at Worzalla, Stevens Point, WI USA.
The text typeface is Abadi Condensed Extra Bold.
The illustrations in this book were created in acrylic paint on canvas.
www.holidayhouse.com
5 7 9 10 8 6 4

Library of Congress Cataloging-in-Publication Data
Pulver, Robin.
Nouns and verbs have a field day / by Robin Pulver;
illustrated by Lynn Rowe Reed. — 1st ed.
p. cm.
Summary: When the children in Mr.Wright's class have a field day,
nouns and verbs in the classroom make their own fun.

ISBN-10: 0-8234-1982-7 (hardcover)
ISBN-13: 978-0-8234-1982-1 (hardcover)

[1. Schools—Fiction. 2. Contests—Fiction.
3. English language—Noun—Fiction.
4. English language—Verb—Fiction.]
I. Reed, Lynn Rowe, ill. II. Title.

PZ7.P97325Nou 2006
[E]—dc22   2005046207

ISBN-13: 978-0-8234-2097-1 (paperback)

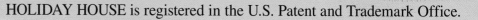

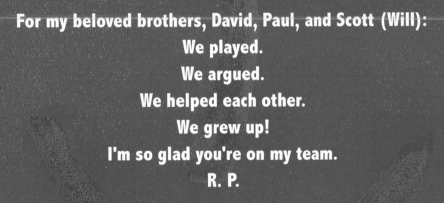

For my beloved brothers, David, Paul, and Scott (Will):
We played.
We argued.
We helped each other.
We grew up!
I'm so glad you're on my team.
R. P.

To my mother, Gloria Rowe,
whose keen interest in my work is always endearing
and only sometimes annoying
L. R. R.

Where the action is

Each day in Mr. Wright's classroom, the kids searched the room for nouns and verbs.

Always reach for the stars.

Nouns are names for people, places, and things.

Verbs are where the action is.

But one morning Mr. Wright announced,
"No time for nouns and verbs today.

It's Field Day!"

"Hooray!" shouted the kids, and they raced outside.

The door slammed behind them, leaving the nouns and verbs all aflutter. The words felt sentenced to a long, boring day without the kids. What's Field Day? they wondered.

"Look!"
said a verb.

"Window!"
said a noun.

The words looked
out the window and
saw the kids on the
playground.

"Run, jump, hop, throw," said the verbs. "Play!"

"Games, races, contests," said the nouns.

"Listen!" said a verb.

They heard kids whooping and hollering and laughing.

"FUN!" said a noun.

The nouns and verbs wanted to play too.
They wanted to have as much fun as the kids,
so they decided to have their own field day.

"Teams! Pairs!"
said some nouns.

"Choose!"
said a verb.

When they
picked teams,
the nouns chose
other nouns.

Verbs wanted to be with other verbs.

Push, pull, yank, **and** tow **said they belonged together.**

Hop, skip, **and** jump **chose one another.**

push

PULL

tow

yank

HOP

skip

jump

Shout
**wanted to be
with** cheer.

Throw **and**
catch **refused to
be separated.**

So did chew
and eat.

custodian

We have so much in

caterp

Long nouns were happiest
with other long nouns.

Pronouns stayed together,
waiting their turn.

he   it   us

she   we

Proper nouns
made sure their team's name started with capital letters.

Finally the leader shouted, "*Get ready, get set, go!*"

The nouns got ready. But they were helpless without the verbs.

The verbs got set. But they couldn't do anything without the nouns.

The nouns and verbs stared at one another. More than ever they felt sentenced to a long, boring day without the kids. They were frustrated and sad and mad.

Finally they looked out the window again.

Outside, Sam ran. Jacinta hopped.

Mike and Ting were throwing and catching.

Kids were pulling and tugging

and falling down!

YEA!

Mr. Wright cheered.

"We forgot . . . ," yelled a verb.

". . . our jobs!" shouted a noun.

"Things happen when we work TOGETHER!"

"We need verbs!" said the nouns.

"We need nouns!" said the verbs.

Then they chose new teams and partners so they could have fun and play their own games.

Then, "Get ready, get set, GO!" The nouns and verbs kicked off their own field day.

Nouns and verbs played tug-of-words.

Nouns and verbs

played hide-and-seek.

Simon says
spin around.

Simon
says
jump.

jUmP

N

**Nouns and verbs played
Simon Says.**

Kiss the
fish!

oops

kiss

Nouns chose partners for the three-legged race.

book + worm = **bookworm**

sun + fish = **goldfish**

moon + log = **blackboard**

Then the new compound nouns teamed up with verbs.

"We need you!"

Nouns acted out verbs for the others to guess.

The nouns and verbs had the time of their lives.

Finally they decided to show Mr. Wright's class how much fun nouns and verbs could be.

They made up new games for the kids.

twist

juggle

MATH

and juggled

and twisted.

They scrambled

HELLO?

LAUGH

They laughed themselves silly.

When Mr. Wright's class came back, the kids couldn't believe their eyes.

the stars reach for Always.

"Wow!" they said. "Nouns and verbs moved around!"

The over jumped moon. the cow

Mr. Wright looked puzzled. "I forgot to close the window. It must have been the breeze."

But when Mr. Wright and his kids noticed the message on the board, they couldn't wait to have a different kind of field day,

Dear _____ ,   (Choose a noun: caterpillar, balloon, kids, lunch)

You can _____   (Choose a verb: eat, play, erase, ride)
around with verbs
and nouns.

Your _____ ,   (Choose a noun: wastebasket, fruit cup, bathroom, friends)
Nouns and Verbs

the end

Kids Can Play Around with Nouns and Verbs

Tongue Twister

Announcing: Nouns! Nouns are known for naming. Names are nouns and nouns are names. Know what nouns are naming now?

Tongue Twister

Active verbs are busy words so don't disturb the busy verbs.

Verb Verse

You'll need to know this for the quiz: Verbs are where the action is!

Match up these nouns to make compound nouns.

bull	**ship**
friend	**house**
cup	**ball**
dog	**frog**
basket	**cake**

Which of these verbs can also be nouns?

watch	**ride**
fan	**ring**
kid	**saw**
fall	**fly**
kiss	

(Answer: all of them!)

When do two verbs equal a noun?

When see + saw = seesaw